Joseph Hodgson

Rhymes on intemperance

Joseph Hodgson

Rhymes on intemperance

ISBN/EAN: 9783337272012

Printed in Europe, USA, Canada, Australia, Japan

Cover: Foto ©Andreas Hilbeck / pixelio.de

More available books at **www.hansebooks.com**

RHYMES

—ON—

INTEMPERANCE

—BY—

JOSEPH HODGSON.

Author of "Poetic Musings."

Thayer Co. Sentinel Print.

HEBRON, NEB.

CONTENTS.

PREFACE.

Let us ask ourselves the question, Is there to all mankind a vested interest in each other's moral, intellectual, and even physical perfection? If so, how much, in this point of view, does intemperance injure us—injure not only ourselves, but our neighbors, our fellow-citizens, and countrymen?

We all know that the vile traffic in stimulants affords a living unto a few; these few too lazy-willed and mean-souled to act honorably, and try to obtain it after a more approved and honest manner.

These very few derive living profits by creating a sort of misery, by engendering vice and poverty, which others, or the public charity, is taxed to support. Then to clap the cap and climax of folly on government, a few lazy, mean souls are licensed to do this at the expense of the general welfare of society.

The people's morals become depraved, their intellect debased and restrained from development, and their physical condition is greatly injured—all for what? That a few worthless characters and useless drones—aye, a thousand times worse than useless—may acquire a disreputable living.

Oh, that we could enforce prohibition, what improvement might we not expect to see? The poor would have plenty, the jails be empty, the attorneys be turned from the practice of law unto honest labor, useful, producing labor, unto healthy manual labor.

The author here of these few Intemperance Rhymes, being a cripple, asks the patronage of the good and benevolent. The cheerful, ready purchaser can have his hearty thanks, and need not expect to be a loser while benefiting himself as well as others.

Rose Creek, Thayer Co., Neb., March 22, 1880.

INTRODUCTORY RHYME.

I am a little book ;
   My author took some pains
That others might with pleasure look
   Into my letter'd brains,
To find out what amuse
   And all of real worth
They could obtain from my peruse
   To praise my merits forth.

But am afraid, afraid,
   Some will not value me,
Nor care ev'n were the author dead
   Who did create to be.
Oh! that I were a glass—
   A glass of ruby wine,
Or whiskey dram—how soon, alas!
   They'd taste me for a DIME.

Nor would they call me *dear*,
   Nor say I was *not good*,
Nor worth a *dime* their souls to cheer,
   Or 'rouse their rabid blood.
But brief would be their glory,
   When I was swallow'd down,
For it would be the sad *old story*
   Of drunken, bad renown.

Then had I better be,
   Just what you see and read—
An admonition *verily*
   To those who counsel need ;

To show their dangerous folly
  Who drink, and drink, and drink,
Till whiskey drives them melancholy
  Upon rough ruin's brink.   .

THE VICE SALOON.

What is a vice saloon?   A thing
  To grip and hold the human soul,
Like some mechanic's tool, and bring
  Fast under Satan's strong control.

What is a vice saloon?   A dam
  Upon life's river, which should flow
Onward before the great I AM.
  Undamag'd by such depths of woe.

What is a vice saloon?   A leech
  Upon the hand of love and health,
A tap on strength, which ought to teach
  How soon we may lose all of wealth.

What is a vice saloon?   A curse
  To every woman, man and child;
For ever making humans worse,
  Their language more and more defil'd.

What is a vice saloon?   A hell
  In minature upon the earth,
Where rowdy drunkards love to dwell,
  To spit their spleen, and martyr mirth.

The vice saloon's a place to pour
  A vial full of human woes,
To make a drunkard every hour
  Who fast the road of ruin goes.

Behold ! in these saloons, the reign
　　Of ill, where man on man will frown
Intoxicated ; rob for gain
　　Till God in judgment sharp looks down.

Why can not mortals, thoughtful, let
　　The cursed things of evil be ;
Pluck no forbidden fruit, but get,
　　And only get, what right they see.

Behold ! that useful pump, a thing
　　To draw cool water from the earth,
A sober sense of blessing bring,
　　Superior to ungodly mirth.

To draw it with a gentle hand,
　　A cheerful mind, a right good-will ;
And at the same time nobly stand
　　A creature free from vice and ill.

Away with vice saloons ! away
　　With all that here destroys the soul,
Ruins the mind, doth reason slay ;
　　Away with tools of Satan all.

'pril 19, 1878.

DRUG SALOONS.

On earth, lo ! hell and heaven between,
　　Of man, the work of his self will,
Is found full many a strangest scene—
　　Full many a place of human ill.

See drunkard, drug and law saloons,
　　And places for religious cant,
Where, changing with the changing moons,
　　Men seek whate'er their humors want.

What is a drug saloon?   A place
   Licensed to deal in things of hell,
To look on man with wolfish face,
   Sheep-clad, to do ill to do well.

A drug saloon is full of jars,
   Glass jars with medicinal things,
Too frequent use of which oft mars
   The health which nature kindly brings.

With thoughtless mind, wend not your way
   Unto those places, lest you have
Too often for such drugs to pay,
   Till you become their very slave.

Oh! do not call on drug saloons,
   To often fill an empty flask,
To feel so luny with the moons,
   As reformation is a task.

Drink is a tempter to the weak,
   An appetizer to the strong;
Who fondly will with folly seek—
   The road to ruin is not long.

But what is ruin? can you tell?
   Something more strong than rum or wine;
It is a state in which to dwell,
   Where misery lives or conscience whines.

A place where vanity and pride;
   No use of vain presumptions find
A state where rolls a lava tide,
   Of flame-like feelings o'er the mind.

Oh! these saloons are hells own gate,
   The drugs they sell just kill the soul;
Fire it as with the match of fate,
   Until it burns beyond control.

Away with all such ruinous things,
   Away with pleasures causing pain,
Away with drugs whence misery springs,
   As neither fit for swine or men.

ril 29, 1878.

DO NOT TREAT.

Do not treat because you love,
Otherwise your friendship prove,
Though of right good social cheer,
Do not treat for friendship here.

When is danger in the cup
That in redness bubbles up;
When is danger where you stand
With temptation in your hand.

Oh receive not friendships smile
Drinking here's good health the while,
With some spirits mean and vile
When is danger, where is guile.

Taste not then the sparkling wine,
Call not Whiskey's goblet fine;
You may stagger ere you doubt,
And from friendship fall clean out.

You may tipple, snuff and smoke,
You may idle, trifle, talk;
'Till you step on ruin's ledge,
Come to want in hoary age,

Without prudence in your plan
To be cautious all you can,
You may step by step come down
Under adversity's dark frown.

Midst the checker'd scenes of life,
When there is a look of strife;
Temperance is a useful thing,
Unto friendship closely cling.

Heading not a telling wink,
How you thoughtlessly may sink,
You may get a sudden fall,
Death may pounce upon your soul.

Love your neighbor, self and God,
By adhering to the good ;
By refusing drunkard's treat,
Love is sweet without more sweet.

Though the glass may sparkle fine,
Ruby red may be the wine;
Though a friend's a friend indeed,
Do not taste, you have no need.

Act with forethought, seeking good ;
Ever fear the eye of God;
Be ye wise in time, and prove
That you do sincerely love.

Live, by loving all you can,
On the christian's noble plan ;
Love with prayer instead of wine,
Grandest treat is love divine,

February 10, 1878.

THE TRUMPET BLOWN.

1 looked, and I saw a mighty angel, blowing his
trumpet unto the nations, warning them against the
sin of drunkenness.

And I stood upon a mountain,
  Lovely valleys were below,
Many a sweetly-flowing fountain,
  Through the valleys wander'd slow.

And I looked each way, and every
  Which the winds of heaven could blow,
Saw some men were full of knavery,
  Others full of want and woe.

And I saw, a mighty angel
  On this earth, God's footstool stand;
And I heard, his trumpet sounding;
  Which did sound to every land.

And I heard it sounding loudly,
  Drunkards that do God forget;
(As he blow'd, it sounded clearly),
  Are a vile rebellious set.

Set against his worthy kingdom,
  Set against his righteous rule;
Like the wild ass acting wildly,
  Wilful, like the stubborn mule.

Set against all social order,
  Set against the public good;
And against heaven's holy border
  Kicking oft, and hard withstood.

Quarreling oft, and rudely bawling,
  Bawling out their sin and shame;
Hellward rushing, downward rolling,
  Soul and body all aflame.

All athirst for ardent spirits,
　　All aglow with fierce desire ;
Which they may by birth inherit,
　　Or, by habit more acquire.

These can never, never enter.
　　Nor come nigh yon lofty gates ;
But will God forsaken venture
　　Where the devil only lets.

As forgetting that their being
　　Should not God. and love disown ;
As forgetting the all-seeing
　　Would have glory and renown.

Would have men never gainsay him,
　　Conscious of his right and good ;
Wicked those who disobey him,
　　And their folly, understood.

Lets them into every error,
　　Lets them boldly curse and drink ;
Lets them without thought, or terror,
　　Lower fall and deeper sink.

For their lusts so very sensual,
　　For their ways so devious all,
For their appetites so beastly.
　　Under condemnation fall.

Pride and folly that are ever
　　Eating of forbidden fruit ;
Full of guile, and false endeavor,
　　Only act themselves to suit.

Bad examples unto others,
　　Tempt and lead the evil way ;
Carelessly will draw their brothers,
　　Far from virtues path astray.

Wicked as the fiendish murderer,
  Selfish as the midnight thief;
The drunkard acts like reckless gambler,
  He of sinners is the chief.

God will punish every drunkard,
  They shall find out that he wills
Qualms, and pains, and tears for folly;
  Self-will'd pleasures all are ills.

Who have with the foulest acids,
  Drugg'd, and poison'd fellowmen;
God will act to them implacid,
  And shall spoil their worthless gain.

Who have done so much injury?
  Who have made the orphans cry?
God will look on them with fury,
  Then shall turn away his eye.

Thus did blow the mighty angel;
  And I look'd again and saw,
That man's oonscience grew more tender,
  As more clearly he did blow.

Till his thoughts grew hot within him,
  Stirr'd by conscience like a rod;
Till he owned he was a rebel,
  And a sinner against God.

Oct. 31, 1875. ————

THE LIQUOR WAR.

We've a sad, old drunkard here,
  Who seems feeling rather queer;
Like to shed the unwonted tear,
  O'er the question, wine and beer—
    All for folly.

What the world with him's the matter,
　With his teeth so prone to clatter,
With his eyes so apt to water,
　　With his tongue to hate bespatter—
　　　O, by golly!

'Tis, he now begins to think,
　That he can not have his drink,
And, in carnal pleasures sink,
　　Means and money for a blink—
　　　And be jolly.

'Tis the liquor license here,
　One big thousand for the year,
Fills him full of dread and fear,
　　Drives him without hope of beer—
　　　Melancholy.

With his feelings highly tensed,
　He is strongly up against,
All the men who have commenced,
　　While the women have condensed—
　　　The Liquor War.

And he spatters out amain,
　Spits his words like drops of rain,
Calls the question up again,
　　As he felt it gave him pain—
　　　Or, some jar.

But he could be cured well,
　If his faith he did not sell,
In Christ Jesus, let me tell,
　　Love for all men would prevail—
　　　Near and far.

Soon like blazes, news would run,
  That the drunkard had been won,
To wisely evil manners shun,
  Had a brighter course begun—
    Like a star.

From the drunkard's harden'd nature,
  Chang'd to lovely, handsome feature,
Rebel of gigantic stature,
  Turn'd into a humble creature—
    All by grace.

Thus the sinner may be made,
  Better seen than can be said;
Thus the inebriate may have aid,
  By the Holy Spirit led—
    In a race

To endure, his foe to beat,
  Favor'd with the saints to meet,
Round the Father's mercy seat,
  Where his own each other greet—
    Hopeful case!

When the liquor is debar'd,
  From transgressor's ways so hard;
Thus the drunkard may be starr'd,
  Looking ever heavenward—
    With his face.

Nov. 20, 1875.

REPLY TO THE "TRAMP PRINTER."

IN SAME STYLE AS HIS.

Poor old tramp,
  And vagrant scamp,

Tramping so through ice and snow.
　　Thou shouldst have pain
　　In heart and brain
Who no better sense canst show.

　　Than just to tramp
　　Through cold and damp
Reckless, heedless on forever,
　　Without the wit
　　To get a sit,
Or, once to make a good endeavor.

　　No sit, ye bet,
　　Such tramp will get
In this world with life so short ;
　　Who e'er squanders
　　Time, and wanders
Here and there, a drunken sport.

　　Rich and proud
　　In every crowd.
Should be glad to let him go,
　　Though he sigh
　　And think of pie (pi),
Hungry, weak, and craven so.

　　Here, hear old tramp
　　Of villain stamp
Friendship is a dying ember ;
　　Without love
　　To rightly prove
Something worthy to remember.

"Professional villains take their ease,"
　　Art thou then villain unprofest ;
"Hypocrites pray on bended knees"
　　But must thou tramp to make request.

"Roam. roam
Away from home"
Out of reason, out of bread ;
Drinking oft
Brain become soft,
And never worth a single "red."

True there be those in every hall
Who'd drink and dance forever ;
And while they live with merry soul,
Will of religion think never.

The great I AM, who is just in his love,
Has given the law such neighbors to prove;
And if like a tree no good fruit they bear
He will try them full soon with "compass
and square."

Love can not forgive, nor justice reprieve,
Those who, e'er thoughtless, in folly will
live;
A place in heaven they never can share,
When tried by the Rule "with compass and
square."

The old tramp's days will not be many more,
But dead drunk he may pass to the unseen
shore.
And, I AM, though merciful, yet fair,
"Will try the old tramp with compass and
square."

And one that will drink, will eat and not pay,
Will send from his presence forever away ;
No excuse for the one that would not do fair,
When tried and found out "with compass
and square,"

Dec. 12, 1875,

FPITAPH.

ON A TAILOR, NAMED —— LYNCH, AND WELL KNOWN
TO THE AUTHOR.

Here lyeth Lynch, whom whiskey lynch'd,
Though he from whiskey never flinch'd,
  When wildly on the spree ;
Excepting when he got too full
Of drugs and acids, beyond rule
  Of love and equity.

When conscious sober, he was wise
With skillful hands and eager eyes,
  To cut fine cloths and new :
Ready to measure any man,
And dress him out on fashions plan,
  As fast as he could sew.

When drunk, he look'd a little hazed,
His tongue would wag, his brains were crazed.
  His wit came wildly out ;
He found he could not keep it in,
For drink makes sense and reason thin
  Without a shade of doubt.

He worked hard, he charged high,
Made money fast with evil eye,
  To gain the world's dross ;
But so illused it when he got
Himself abused, and made a sot,
  That it all went to loss.

He lived so foolish, as most men
Appear to do, and he was vain
  Of things so worldly small.
The drunkard spends his manhood's prime,
And oft his life's appointed time
  As if more beast than soul,

He lived as though believing Christ
His life had never sacrificed
  For sinners all so vile;
No heaven to well reward the saint,
No place of endless banishment.
  No faith creed worth his while.

He lived in folly long enough
Was weak to try reform, was proof
  against all good advice;
Yes, he was weak, an abject slave
Of alcohol, and never brave
  Enough to conquer vice.

Yet he was free and social kind,
Then think of him with pitying mind,
  And softly drop a tear;
For now he lies with full closed eyes,
Where he no more can whiskey prize
  Nor drink besotting beer.

Though thoughtful tears roll down the cheek,
That he like us was frail and weak,
  And came no nearer heaven;
He found at last what nature craves
For all, where long the green grass waves,
A place to sleep, a mortal's grave,
  From vice and folly driven.

  Come drop a tear,
  Poor Lynch lies here.

Peace to his ashes, may his soul
Rest where no waves of trouble roll,
  May God forgive him now.
And if he can not enter heaven,
No lower may his soul be driven,
  But calm rest on his brow,

Nov, 28, 1875.

THE CONTRAST.

Behold the difference, lasting great, extreme,
Betwixt the real good, and folly's dream,
To shun the waste of days, and months, and
    years,
For, time improv'd a lasting boon confers;
See, moralizing Christians still essay,
For happiness and virtue day by day,
By choosing sober paths thro' this rough
    world,
Beneath their Banner truthful wide unfurl'd
They march in bands of union, order, strength
And thus expect to reach their home at length.
Their fathers home with all their sins for-
    given,
Beyond this changeful scene, in yonder
    Heaven.

Again, behold the drunkard, ragg'd and tired,
Unslept, unblest, his company undesir'd,
Excepting where the person takes him in,
Who gives him drink in foul exchange for tin.
Midst midnight brawls he rushes into crime,
Endangers life, far worse than wastes his
    time.
His children cry for bread, yet naught he
    hears,
Naught save his vile companion's roar and
    rant;
No family distress his heart can daunt,
Or, stop him in his wretched, mad career,
He dies, and misery is his record here,

THE CIGAR.

Out, out on that silly thing, that dark brown
    cigar,
Ye dandified gentles so fondly prefer,
What hours at a tavern it giveth employ,
Amid gluttons that puff with a relish of joy.

With a square-flipp'd cap, and brisk-looking
    physog,
  Your "broth of a boy" is a figure incog,
Who whistles at pleasure and lights his cigar,
Disgraceful to man at the publican's bar.

Oh! where does the column of majesty
    stand,
When reason asserts her supremacy grand,
And reigns over mind with the sceptre of
    truth,
For ever to banish the follies of youth.

Oh! not in the usage inferior by far,
Of lighting up thought with a smoking cigar;
But better when error, as blue curling smoke,
Must vanish in air like a lack lustre joke.

Oh! great is the fear of a dark brown cigar,
That fires up a village more furious than
    war,
When thoughtlessly thrown in a corner aside,
Since tickling the taste of some whimsical
    pride.

Hark! hark to the shout of the fireman loud,
Look, look at the rush of the anxious crowd;
Gaze, gaze on the scene of the wild-leaping
    flames,
Fierce tongues of the fire which confusion
    proclaims.

What matter, what matter, a dark brown cigar,
See! foul-mouth'd presumption will ever prefer;
Then light up a one that with folly consumes,
To see all the doers of ill to their tombs.

Ye cities! your plaint must to heaven ascend,
Ere man of his folly e'er seeketh to mend;
Ere, heaven-assisted, he probeth the cause,
Whence often the tide of calamity flows.

THE TAVERN.

The tavern never can suffice
   To please, when conscience often calls;
A tavern's noise, that house of vice,
   Will never do for humble souls.

The place of guilt, of sin, of wrong,
Of midnight mirth, of comic song;
Where goodness ever flies the door,
Where haggard care walks o'er the floor;
Affords no rest, offers no hope,
For man with sorrow e'er to cope.

The place obscene, with dirty rags,
Where idleness for ever lags,
Which squalid poverty imports,
Where impudence again retorts.
Where many a fleeting health is drunk,
And oft the passing coin is sunk,
All to no purpose here on earth,
Except to cause of joy more dearth.

Ye wretched scenes of vice and evil,
Of violence, threatenings, words uncivil,
Of boisterous joys, of aimless rant,
Of thoughtless wit, of absurd cant.
Ye are too vain to tempt my stay,
From scenes like these I must away.

The humble soul can never brook,
The proflicate's obdurate look ;
His joys ungrounded, hope's delusions,
His haunts of misery, sad confusions ;
His vices which so little please,
With conscience often ill at ease;
Whene'er he looks upon the good,
Whene'er he thinks upon his God—
Whose follies lead to endless ruin,
With judgment in their path pursuing.

Ye scenes of passion's lawless moods,
Where care is drown'd in foaming floods ;
Where love departs from all that's good,
Where folly's children hatch and brood
The ills of life; and, where the soul
Beneath the power of alcohol.
Is brought into a vile subjection,
To clank the chains of low connection ;
To sow the seeds of certain crime,
To raise the weeds, not flowers of time ;
To crush the tho'ts that seek to rise,
With heavenly hopes to starry skies.

Ye scenes disgusting, dramas rude,
Of life theatrical, the balls
Which custom haunts, where fashion calls ;
Where prudence never may intrude,

Your reign is horrible, your dens
Of infamy no lust restrain.
Away, from scenes like these, away !
Ye are too bad to tempt my stay.
Jan. 18, 1862.

TOBACCO.

Away with ye fumes of tobacco and smoke,
  Ye delusions so vain
  On the senses of men ;
Let me breath of the clear and refreshing
 sweet air,
To inhale to my lungs all again and again,
  What only is pure,
  That health may endure,
What only is good for the spirit of man,
Since pleasures habitual to evil illure.

Ye loved impositions, can reason allow ?
  These much relish'd desires
  Of the pipe's kindled fires.
They are hurtful, expensive and useless to
 you.
Give me those wholesome things which my
 nature requires ;
  Things good for the mind,
  All the wisdom ye find ;
What ever promotes the well being of all,
The good disposition ever welcome and as
 kind.
West Allendale, England, 1847.

TOBACCO.

Ye fumes of dark tobacco, 'way with you
    away!
Ye are the smoke that 'scends from where the
    devils stay;
Ye are the tiny clouds which hide men's little
    faults.
Until the devils drag them to the infernal
    vaults.
Thou vile tobacco, stinkenist weed, offshoot
    of hell,
That has taken root on earth, and grows, ah,
    grows too well,
Like alcohol oft used, to shortens life's brief
    span;
As other vices which engross the mind of
    man,
Through will'd forgetfulness of nature, na-
    ture's God,
And all his holy laws which guide on heaven's
    road,
Thou'rt here, and cultivated well with Folly's
    care,
To lead the thoughtless from those scenes
    most bright and fair;
And, by what engine foul, drawn thro' the
    mouth of man,
Invention without wit; and void of wisdom's
    plan;
Clay made, fill'd full, and lighted up with fire
    and air,
To puff vile fumes, and poison pleasure every-
    where.
Oh, dark tobacco, charm for care that oft is
    sought,

Thou type of weakness, vanity and human
    thought,

From vice habitual drawn to error's endless
    night;

In spite of nature's God who sai 1, " let there
    be light,"

And light was, and is, o'er all the fair and
    flowery earth,

Where sure God never meant tobacco to have
    birth

Except for herbal use, a medicinal cause,

(How blest is he that herbal lore and uses
    knows).

But man, hear reason say, it never was de-
    sign'd

For him to use in all the various forms ye
    find,

Of plug, of twist, of shagg, and mouth-
    cock'd hot cigars ;

In all those forms it hath its victims like the
    wars.

So purely poisonous and pernicious is the
    weed,

Whoever use, had better only smoke indeed.

Whoever chews it much, will, without any
    doubt,

Soon spit, spit much, and spit his constitution
    out.

Oh surely God created not the weed to kill,

But meaning it some useful purpose to fulfil ;

Not in the common way, so foul, so vile, so
    mean,

Oh ! never in a way so dirty and obscene.

Again, oh ! once again, lets hear what reason
    says,

So wise in counsel and experienced in her
    ways;
She shows how prone is man to waste his
    coin and time
In learning folly, doing evil, touching crime,
Tasting forbidden fruit, and wandering oft
    amiss,
Far thro' this wide, wide world's weary
    wilderness.

Canada, 1862.

RUM.

THE RAPID TRANSIT ROUTE TO JAIL.

Too much of drink makes sorry drunk,
Strong rum o'ercomes the human soul,
    Soon care is drown'd, and hope is sunk,
Thoughtless intemperance ruins all.

Strong liquor fires the very blood,
Yea, sets the soul on fire of hell;
    Out of *bad* whiskey comes no good,
Except confinement in some jail.

If any jail-bird, often flown,
Is better e'er for being confin'd;
    If good desire has stronger grown,
To keep possession of the mind.

Such birds as these, which must be
    eaged,
To keep from mischief, vice, and harm;
    How ever oft to temperance pledg'd,
Are apt again to meet with harm.

Too prone to fall the same ill way,
To warm their passions, heat up, fell;
    Rum is to sinners, jolly gay,
"The rapid transit rout to jail."

Till often for their failings here,
Who ask for sins to be forgiven;
    There comes no other better cheer,
A chariot, but not from heaven.

The wicked never can do well,
With aims so mean, ways always wrong,
    That run the sinner into hell,
To try his hard endurance long.

Forsaken by the friend of man,
Forgotten by the living all;
    With misery in the burning pan,
Conscience tormenting still the soul.

Oh! let us ever pity, then
The thoughtless drunkard, thus consum'd;
    For want of love shown unto men,
Who is to misery always doom'd.

"Man's inhumanity to man"
Sells liquor, mix'd with want and woe,
    For sake of gain, an evil plan,
Which many wink at, tho' they know.

The Christian may be much profess'd,
The pulpit often occupied,
    Ev'n Sinners pray'd to, and address'd,
But *how much* practice here e'er has lied?

Wake up! wake up! ye son's of men,
Let reason stablish only right,
    Banish the wrong, the mean, the vain,
But keep humanity in sight.

Aug. 10, 1878.

AN ELEGY.

[The supposed Lament and Reflections of Mr. Gordon on the death of his Mare Bessy].

O Bessy's dead, our own good mare,
And heavy is my heart with care;
When threshing, how at Mr. Lee's,
The *terror* did upon her sieze;
Her sore affliction, pain, and death
Came o'er me like a thing of stealth,
Beat down my head, my mind to toss,
Weigh'd on my heart a heavy loss.

Yes, Bessy's dead, my hope, my care,
Relations must affliction share;
Living, she was a real gain,
But dead, she yields me naught but pain,
She was a friend whom all might need,
A docile, free, and mettled steed
As need to walk upon a road,
A cheerful puller of a load.
So strong, so true, so good to draw,
She was a friend without a flaw,
A useful aid in many a way,
A steady help on many a day,
A noble beast—who less would say?

Amidst the throng, the hours of toil
It almost made my mind recoil,
With cool and sad reflection's check,
From all its free extension back—
Back to a dearth of every joy,
Nay, it had almost made me cry;
The big round tear stood in mine eye,
For sad was I her woe to see,
That e'er we thus should parted be
From friendship, labor, hope and gain,
Oh! who his grief could *now* refrain,

Yes, Bessy's dead!—while working well
   Death's cruel hands shot forth an arrow,
Who should essay the cause to tell,
   Where partial reasons are too narrow.

She lived to feed—she bled to die,
With inflamation running high.

'Tis thus the drunkard, thoughtless weight,
In ruins pleasure doth delight,
And deepest draughts doth fearless take,
Till all his limbs with palsy shake,
Strong rum will set the soul on fire,
And cherish many a wrong desire;
While every drink brings thirst again,
Unquench'd his thirst doth aye remain;
Bound is his soul, body and all,
That downwards to destruction roll,
In habits adamantine chain,
To suffer loss, and grief, and pain.
Thus oft we see man in the way
Of stupid folly go astray.

Who loves to drink each heavy tide,
   That laves the shores of life,
Who loves to feed the lust of pride
   Where sin and death are rife,
Defiles his Maker's image, sinks
   The human in the brute,
But at the judgment 'pending, winks
   To taste the bitter fruit;
He plucks not from the tree of life
   Sweet immortality,
But eats the fruit of care and strife,
   And riots carnally.

His pulse beats fast with fever high,
And fiery red each blood shot eye;
Surfeited oft to sicken. die;
Who eats too much, and thinks too little,
Chews, smokes, snuffs, drinks, e'ven wastes
    his spittle.

The slave of vice and folly,
He eyes the world with looks of pleasure,
And time takes always at his leisure,
Knows nothing of that fairer treasure
    That tender melancholy,
By good men loved, those truly great
In soul, who can anticipate
The full enjoyment, free from fate,
Of Heaven's eternal, happy state;
But topes and wassails beyond measure,
To fail at last beneath the pressure
    Of God and nature's retribution,
Down-trodden 'neath the verdant sod;
Who always walks the sinner's road,
    Ne'er makes on earth a restitution
For gifts and mercies he has got,
He shall be cursed woe be his lot.
Though insect like his fancies play
A little while, a sunny day,
Like butterfly so passing gay,
Which flies without a wish to stay
From flower to flower, from spray to spray,
Till sickness blasts its life away.

But he must render up account
    For moments gone to waste,
Or suffer to the full amount
    A conscience of unrest.

Who revels here in a wicked sphere,
Nor heeds that there's enthron'd on high
A God with an all-seeing eye,
A God who long hath mercy shown,
To whom his weaknesses are known,
Who long his judgment hath foreborne,
Midst his wild career of scorn.

The drunkard cries another glass,
    When, hark! a voice in dreadful tone
Pale death appears, he dies, alas!
    Where is he gone?

O where the would be Christian tends,
In worldly-mindedness he ends;
He drinks too deep of carnal things,
He pulls too hard at Mammon's strings;
He lives for gain, he hoards in doubt,
Till life's short lease in Death runs out.
Behold him sit at heaven's door,
'A houseless soul' most abject, poor.
There is to him who hath not wisely strive
No hope of rest, no invitation given.
No door of mercy opens wide,
The soul that sins what woes betide;
Fix'd irrevocable is his doom,
Death shrouds his soul in endless gloor
Then let the glutton mark his care,
The wretched miser watch his share,
For full surfeit, or penurious fare,
Let such beware of many a snare:
For Bessy's dead, our own good mare!
And heavy is my heart with care,—
Oh! would not for a hundred dollars
She thus had died, oh! gloomy colours,

Oh! murky shades, oh vain ambitions!
Oh joys soon fled, oh dear delusions!
How oft ye warp the mind of man,
How oft ye darken o'er his span,
How oft ye sieze his little joys
And leave him naught but groans and
    sighs;
Since Bessy's dead, our own good mare.
A faithful friend whoe'er would gain,
She died, but ne'er to live again;
When joy wakes not, what hopes are vain.
Though hope might ne'er, might ne'er
    despair,
Yet give me wings to fly from care.
For adverse fortune cruelly casts
Her with'ring influence in this hour,
Like Boreas' cold, wintry blasts
Amidst the snow's descending shower;
The flakes of snow descend and hide
The precious life-blood's crimson tide,
Forth issuing from an open vein.
The skilful farrier tries in vain
To probe the cause, the life blood flows,
But inflamation, fever, pain
Have stretch'd her nerves, no more to
    strain.
Those swollen limbs ne'er will draw again.
Methought she might have been a stay
To lighten toil and care away.
How oft is man in prospect cheated,
On which he builds his hopes conceited;
How oft they fail ere half completed,
Change of views, him only leaving.
What once was joy is care annoying,

What once was loved is peace destroying;
This comes of all of earth's alloying;
Giving him much cause for grieving;
And ah! this oft dispels the dreams
That haunt the brain of mortal man;
This comes of ill-concerted schemes,
·Which to project is all we can.
How oft, too oft, we mortals find,
With bosom fears, and troubled mind,
Our future prospects all confin'd,
With clouds before and storm behind.
But what can sorrow e'er avail,
Which words can ne'er suffice to tell,
When language fails, when tears are shed.
Grief must prevail; *now Bessy's dead !*

HELPS.

A gentle word of good advice
    Is better than a glass of rum,
Which grips too oft' in ruins vice
    Until the very soul is numb.

A kindly call to needful prayer
    Is better cheer, is greater aid,
To disentangle from the snare
    Of habits by us evil made.

Look up, there is a Friend of youth
    Who with an eye of pity sees
Our every weakness, and in truth
    Sees all our faults, our enemies.

Confess your sins before his face,
    To save you who is standing by;
He has a fountain full of grace,
    To cleanse from all impurity.

February 13, 1878.

Verses written by request, for the Temperance Ban-
er, published, and read before the members of the
'emperance movement at Rose.C.eek city, Nebraska,
'ebruary, 1878.

LADIES' ADDRESS,
To The Young Men.

I.

All we young ladies, howe'er meek
However young, however weak,
Each have an object, 'tis to seek
    A *Hero*, 'till we find one.
One, that is free from every vice,
Will love and harken to advice,
Leave off bad habits, so unnice;
    A noble, good, and kind one.

2.

Yes, want to find a nobleman,
One true to God, and nature's plan,
Willing to work, do all he can
    To aid the Temperance movement.
For life is short, the hours fly fast,
The scenes of youth will soon be passed,
Habits, once formed, through life may last;
    Our object is improvement.

3.

Come all you young men, we would see
If you have got, as from vice free,
The sign of true nobility,
    As each of us would find one.
We do not care for godless wealth,
Nor lying rogues that live by stealth,
Give each an honest soul with health,
    A temperate, good, and kind one.

4.

When such a heaven-sent prize is won,
Our joy in life shall have begun,
With pleasure every thing be done,
  We'll see a great improvement;
Of truth, and justice, we will sing,
To love and friendship closely cling,
Our homes with music then shall ring,
  To praise the Temperance movemen

[By Request.]

GENTLEMEN'S REPLY TO THE LADIES.

1.

Then here we come, so gallant all,
To sign the *Pledge* at Temperance' call,
And say it with the noblest soul,
  To please ye gentle Ladies,
That we will come, that we will go,
Wherever fortune's favors flow
Wherever fortunes breezes blow,
  Twixt Cape Farewell and Cadiz.

2.

And each will act like noblemen.
Living up well to nature's plan,
To please ye Ladies, all we can,
  Looking so like our sisters;
That, each will try a ready hand,
Use every tool he can command,
Like farmers plough and till the land
  To raise the bread and blisters*

---

*Blisters; pieces of meat fried.

3.

That while our homes look clean and neat
That while our bread tastes fresh and sweet,
That we will look and clean our feet
   · Upon the point of duty,
Nor shall we quaff the flowing wine,
When each has love so sweet and fine,
To warm his heart like love divine,
   Or light with smiles of beauty.

4.

While guarded by his word of truth,
To temperance, wisdom, love, and ruth,
Then shall God favor all our youth.
   And bless in special manner,
Each with his Lady, arm in arm,
When Moon and stars shine on the farm.
Will walk, and know there is a charm
   Beneath the Temperance Banner.

THE TWO LOAFERS.

What we differ'd in opinion,
What we quarrel'd for dominion;
Though such thing as foolish fighting,
Only dogs should e'er delight in.

Yet we tore each other furious,
Others seeing thought it curious;
How we thrash'd each other soundly,
Ah! we hated most profoundly.

We had better both been working
Than each other's faces burking,
Better been at home, and sleeping,
Than such blackguard company keepin

When we made too free with whisky,
Drinking deeply soon got frisky;
We on bolder language ventured,
Then at Danger's Gate we enter'd.

Then we look'd no more like foxes,
But began to get some boxes,
How we heav'd, and reel'd, and stumble
And against each other grumbled.

Had we seen with clearest vision,
Free from folly, pride, ambition;
Had we never been refracted,
We had ne'er like monkeys acted.

Had we never been so funning,
Never been so mean, nor cunning,
Never met, nor drank, nor smoked,
We had ne'er so madly talked.

What is left of all our pleasure?
Joy we prized as misers treasure?
What of all our great acquaintance?
Nothing now, but sad repentance!

THE SALOONIST.

The saloon-keeper wishes all
  Would to his counter and take drink ;
The preachers, teachers, every soul
  Himself would prompt them how to think.

To be most social, take a glass,
  To speak him kindly every day ;
And on to whiskey's glory pass,
  The sinner's rapid downward way.

Thus he o'er others seeks control,
  By ruin's very evil plan.
His is a very narrow soul,
  He is a very lazy man.

No love nor goodness does he show,
  No moral grandeur has in view,
Who plunges sinners into woe,
  Their thoughtless folly here to rue.

Is there no punishment for him ?
  Fame breathes for him an evil breath,
His future's clouded, looking dim
  With something worser even than death.

Yes, let him die, to hades sink,
  Who others' ruin only plans,
Who only evil lives to think,
  Him God from mercy justly bans.

March 16, 1880.

THE DRUNKARD.

The quiet of a conscience free,
　　From cause of quarrel or offense,
Is not imperatively to be
　　The drunkard's show of wit or sense.

With many a row and many a fall,
　　Who onward hastens to that bourne,
Where sinks the sin o'er burthen'd soul—
　　But here, oh! never more returns.

SOME CLINCHING THOUGHTS.

The saloonist the drunkard forces
　　Into a lower hell than death,
For whom his everlasting curses
　　Pour forth in ever-burning breath.

How dare you speak of whiskey's glory!
　　Withdraw the curtain from before;
The drunkard tells his own sad story
　　In lamentations o'er and o'er.

Show us a scene in whiskey's parlor:
　　A table stands with glasses on,
Where drunkards show impassion'd valor
　　O'er cards played, money lost and won.

However social his seducer,
　　With manners bland and cunning speech,
He is the drundards worst abuser,
　　Sucking his purse worse than a leech.

Ye money-loving liquor-venders,
　　Hear ye whose children cry for bread;
Why take ye what their father tenders?
　　Oh! give him loaves and clothes instead.

Oh ! give him mercy's kindly look ;
　Oh ! let him feel the force of truth ;
Tell him to read God's holy Book,
　The hope of age and guide of youth.
rch 16, 1880.

_____ . .

ABSTAIN.

Abstain tetotally from wrong,
　Leave bad companions one and all ;
Seek only good to stay among,
　To refine the pleasures of the soul.

Abstain from every evil thing,
　All 'toxial drinks, as they are ill ;
While only evil from them spring,
　To wrong, to wrong they prompt the will.

Be sure, ye thoughtless, idle throng.
　Ye mortals weary of dull life,
To sing the total abstinence song,
　Aloof from scenes with error rife.

Be sure from evil understood
　That you most safely have abstain'd ;
Abstain'd from drink that fires the blood ;
　Taste not, lose not, think what is gain'd.

Evil's no loss while good is gain'd ;
　By keeping out of sinful strife
A noble character's sustain'd ;
　Duty best shows an honest life.

But fired with burning stimulants
　The soul soon feels its hell on earth ;
For drink, for drink it only pants—
　Not things of most enduring worth.

By keeping on the Zion road,
   Evil is passed and good is gain'd;
Duty is done by honoring God;
   Justly is right and truth maintained.

The wise all praise safe abstinence,
   While others good example see;
To appreciate true worth and sense,
   Seeking the best good company.

March 12, 1880.

EPIGRAMS.

I.

Behold within the mean saloon
Full many a whisky-loving sot,
With folly luny every Moon,
All wisdom teached him as forgot.
Who sits to drink, but cannot think
How there he fools away his time,
Who sits to talk, but cannot walk
Where duty done would look sublime.

II.

Behold within a cozy room,
The drunkard's money stak'd-put down;
Ah! soon he finds his fortune's doom
Equals the faro den's renown.
Ah! that is bad, for he feels sad.
He cannot stake another chance;
Drink crazes him, his senses swim,
Around his eye-balls wildly glance.

III.

Man learns bad habits here, because
From merely monkey mean descended;
The animal within him does
Incline him worse than e'er intended,

His folly smokes
As simply jokes
Till precious time and money's wasted.
He random thinks
At reason winks,
Until to want and ruin hasted.

IV.

Man learns bad habits here—because
He, having pluck'd forbidden fruit,
Still loves to taste it, tho' he knows
It may not all his nature suit,
He tastes it still
With perverse will,
Nor God's commandments cares to keep,
But eats and drinks,
And nods and winks
Until in death he falls asleep.

HOW HAPPY ARE THEY.

GERMAN AIR.

How happy are they
Who are walking the way
Of the followers all of the Lord.
Who wisely have chose
The good temperance cause,
And now pledge to live up to their word.

How happy are they
Who its laws still obey
To find joy in the rulings of right,
They find that the road
They are on leads to God
And their hearts in his goodness delight.

How happy are they
Who let reason bear sway,
And refrain from the drunkard's deep drams,
When tempted to drink
Who have grace and can think—
And can sing the sweet joy-giving psalms.

How happy are they
Who in all things obey
The good will of their Savior and Lord ;
Tho' humble in mind
Who are loving and kind
And will others good counsels afford.

They love to behold
Both the young and the old
As delighted to walk in the way—
The way of true right
To increase their delight
And among all the righteous to stay.
March 18, 1880.

_____

THE EVIL USE OF TONGUE.

My muse once more would strike the lyre,
    As she has oft accustom'd sung,
She now would catch poetic fire
    To sing the evil use of tongue.

There's many evils found among
    Mankind, that custom seems to teach,
And one the evil use of tongue ;
    Is not all lying sinful speech ?

Then things of evil often told
    Do not improve our morals here,
But rather tend to make us bold,
    And sometimes buy experience dear.

Too much of tongue is often evil
  Too much of any thing is bad,
Especially when its uncivil
  And apt to make the bosom sad.

The tongue of slander oft is heard,
  As often busy finding fault;
Words soft and kind are more preferr'd
  Than those wing'd like a thunder bolt

When language is abusive coarse,
  With words of fire and oaths obscene,
Retaliation comes in force
  As punishment for being mean.

The tongue, unruly member, by it
  How much is won, maintained, or lost?
It preaches peace, or raises riot
  When feelings into storms are tost.

The tongue's a symbol of the spirit
  Of man, the index of his mind;
A brief outline foretells the merit
  Which may within be well defin'd.

If thou couldst read the human heart,
  Couldst know thy own and neighbor's
    mind;
Thou surely wouldst not cause such smart
  With words uncivil, tho'ts unkind.

Be calm, considerate and wise,
  With caution striving against wrong,
If thou wouldst harken to advise
  Forethoughtful then
      O spare the tongue.

THE WAGGING TONGUE.

—

I. WOMAN'S.

—

Woman's Tongue is seen a wagging,
`   Wagging often, seldom still;
Woman's tongue's so often bragging
    Too much speaking hard and ill.
How so full of blind conceit?
Lovely woman should be sweet,
Humble looking, meek in face,
Show off only modest grace
                    With an aim.

Is conceit not mental weakness?
    Some say woman's very weak,
Is not pride a sort of sickness?
    Do some show with painted cheek
Sickening pride, as strong in folly;
Far too vain for melancholy,
Weak in reason, sick in sin,
In their fancies light and thin—
                    That is them.

When the spirit's very snappish
    How the tongue wags always ill;
Spite of lust, or feelings rapish,
    Kill's the love it should instill.
When the thoughts that in us rise
Blind all beauty from our eyes,
When our feelings make us weep
Beauty only is skin-deep
                    A hem—hem.

Woman's tongue hark vilely wagging,
    Sue says are you jealous Dick?
Woman's tongue so always bragging

If you are I'll leave you quick.
What's the matter with you now?
What's that cloud upon your brow?
Dick says lightning strikes to kill,
And it thunders o'er us still
        All a-flame.

Dick he drinks and cheats and gambles,
  Sue gives parties, feasts and flares;
Dick from home now often rambles,
  Sue she pawns her household wares.
While the lawyers stand around,
While the judge he looks profound,
While the oaths administer'd,
Falsely tell how humans err'd—
        That's the game.

Hark the lawyers loud intoning,
  Madam should be free,
Says the judge midst yawns and groaning
  Write the severance it must be;
Never matter what the Bill,
Comes divorce of devilish will,
Long sour'd milk is worse than none,
Yet some good if but for one
        Choose the same.

With the tongue incessant wagging,
  Comes no good result to men;
Woman's tongue is loosely bragging,
  Is as wicked as its vain;
And the apple that Eve ate
Adam tasted for hard fate;
With the drink which Adam drank
Eve into misfortune sank—
        Morals lame.

But how will it go with Adam,
  If as Mary Walker said,
Rivers run with blood, for Madam,
  With the ballot in her aid.
With mankind in her employ
To assault the walls of Troy,
And for Helen's beauty fair
To deluge the world with care.
                    What a game.

How a wagging tongue will quiver,
  Feeling heated as with shame;
From its power good Lord deliver,
  For it kindles into flame.
Kindles up as we can prove
Not with friendship, truth, and love,
Kindles with a heated breath
Full of hatred, malice, death,
                    Shun the same.

Though a wagon tongue be useful,
  You can put two horses in;
But the wagging tongue abuseful
  Is like some rash two-horse sin;
With its own coarse heavy sway,
In its evil, downward way,
In the darkness of its hour,
In its hate-producing power,
                    And ill fame.

THE WAGGING TONGUE.

II. MAN'S   .

Oh man's tongue is heard a wagging,
  Lord-a-mercy! how it wags,

Vanity is in his bragging,
  As he talks he often brags;—
Looks into his parlor glass,
  Smiles upon the grandest ass
That e'er walk'd the verdant earth
  Since creation had its birth.
                    That is him!

With conceit his eyes a-flashing
  Deep in pride his thoughts are stuck;
In all beauty, love and passion,
  Dower'd with hope, he dreams of luck;
And he hungers for the praise
  Of mankind, and happy days
To triumph above all scorn,
  As to greatest fortune born.
                    Even him.

Weakest wishes' dull romancing,
  What are these the soul to guide?
With no surer aim advancing
  We bemoan our falling pride,
Learn to stoop as feeling humble,
  Or, against the fates to grumble;
Dole out life a little while
  Without fortunes golden smile—
                    Seeing dim.

Human hopes and earthly troubles,
  "Best laid schemes of mice and men;"
Often on each other doubles,
  "Leave us naught but grief and pain"
Leave us little where the surges
  Of mankind their interest urges
Like a great and swelling tide
  Pouring o'er the ocean wide
                    Dark and grim.

Hear man speak among earth's giants,
　　Talk unto the little ones.
Upon self his great reliance
　　But when self is crush'd he moans,
Kings can rule dominions wide
　　Keeping court with power and pride,
But o'er self how few can rule
　　Without finding passion fuel?
　　　　　　　Few, or none.

What is self e'er without spirit?
　　To build up ambition's aim?
What is man here without merit?
　　Hopeless as without a name.
．All the fashion of his face
　　Youth and beauty, love and grace,
Pass like bubbles down time's stream
　　While hope sheds a fitful gleam
　　　　　　　Glancing on.

Little room for wordy bragging
　　Looking through a fleeting hour.
Little cause for tongues a wagging
　　Without honor, love, or power.
To a righteous seeing eye
　　There's no honesty in a lie,
But the heart, the heart deprav'd,
　　Is with every vice enslaved
　　　　　　　Clearly shown.

Some are fond of mind dominion
　　As a belle is fond of dress,
Hear them urging their opinion
　　Wearying with their tediousness.
Hear them in and out of season

Urging every sense and reason
That another may be taught
    How accept the tender'd thought
        As a gem.

How they marshal like an army
    Banded words of vocal might,
And pour forth as if to harm ye
    For the sake of truth and right,
Where they love these would convince
    How they place full confidence;
Where the strength concentred lies
    Of the argument they prize
        Worthy fame.

Oh man's tongue is heard a-wagging
    Running as before the wind,
Vainly, vainly hear him bragging
    Tiny bits of little mind,
Thoughts of earthly vanity,
    Hearts of frail humanity,
Quiver with the moving tongue,
    Rush like rapid stream along
        With an aim.

March 21, 1880.

ALE.

New ale enriches much the blood,
    Still yielding fresh delight,
Is for the health uncommon good
    When always tasted right.

But he who is soon overthrown
    With prudence should make sure,
Should safely let strong ale alone,
    And keep his motives pure.

For with much drink men will get tight
  A feeling like to burst,
That is the deil's supreme delight
  And triumph o'er the just.

What is the use of feeling tight.
  Far better to be loose ;
What is the use of ill delight,
  When better we can choose.

To get mad-drunk is void of sense ;
  Man shows worse than a beast
Who acts with brazen impudence—
  Of evil much possest.

To get red-hot with drinking, and
  Self-deify the sot.
Is most absurd, against command,
  A blot upon man's lot.

To drink, and drink without an aim
  Is the way to do our worst.
Both worse in purse, and worse in fame
  Is doubly bad accurst.

Then let strong ale alone who can,
  O let it safe alone ;
For sadly by it many a man
  Is truly overthrown.

Drown'd in the deep Red Sea of ruin
  Dark waves come rolling round,
No more vain pleasures here pursuing
  On Death's advantage ground.

Let whisky, rum, and ale alone,
    No fierce temptation rouse,
Better to know cold poverty's bone
    Than deep in drink carouse.

July 7, 1879.

_____

THEM TWAIN ARE ONE.

HE.

I hate a scolding woman in toto,
She sings too much the evil use of tongue.

SHE.

I hate a drunken husband in toto,
As quarelsome, smelling of liquor strong.

HE.

Woman that scolds, talks too much like a
    shrewd,
Feels like offending, without love endued,

SHE,

And man that drinks is surely ready set
To take offense, untangling cupid's net.

HE.

But were you not a shrewd, you would like
    love
Be talking *here*, and not to anger move.

SHE.

Oh we are earthly all, to anger given,
We cannot always love, or 'twould be
    heaven.

HE.

By wrangling, sensual nature is increased,
Scolding is neither fit for man nor beast.

SHE.

Drinking is neither fit for man nor beast,
It makes of man a brute, to say the least.

HE.

You speak too devilish sharp, as without
    feeling
All kindly sense, all social love congealing.

SHE.

Because, by drinking you are surely doing
What will to both bring certain woeful ruin.

HE.

I would not drink, but home is not like
    heaven,
When you are scolding, I am done and
    driven.

SHE.

That shows your conscience, as you felt its
    might,
You may be happy yet by doing right.

HE.

You leave off scolding, I will leave off drink-
    ing,
And that will look as right as love a-winking.

SHE.

Agreed, agreed, my honest-hearted fellow,
Love's always right, like apple ripe and
    mellow.

March 22, 1880.

DO AND DO NOT.

O, do not show Almighty weakness!
Show gentle manners, chilklike meekness!
    Passions should not be sported,
    Dangers should not be courted.
O put away your human blindness,
Try using more of loving kindness;
    Actions are mental moulded,
    Judgments after, unfolded,
O be not then thro' folly spiteful,
But climb up nearer scenes delightful;
    There is a heaven of beauty
    In every moral duty,
And there's a time-improving pleasure
Counting all virtue bosom treasure.

Doing the best as truth discerning,
For knowledge teaches various learning,
    Its precepts should be heeded,
    All gardens should be weeded;
The mind needs careful cultivation
To adorn its human habitation,
    O give it good improving
    With spirit kind and loving,
To rise and soar with high ambition
Above its worldly low condition,
    All heavenly things desiring,
    Of faith and hope's inspiring,
With change of heart so happily given
To reach our Father's home in Heaven.

March 17, 1880. ————

TETOTALER AND DRUNKARD.

DIALOGUE.

T.—Will is nothing without thought,
    Cant you think to will aright?

D.—Yes I can, so help me God,
    With thy love, and truth, and light.

T.—But they tell me that you drink
    When in drink is fire of hell

D.—How when drinking it I think
    That I taste it just as well.

T.—Deep as e'er you taste of evil
    Wilful like it will prevail.
    What is stronger than the Devil ?
    What is surer than his Hell ?

D.—But without a little taste
    Now and then our health may fail,
    Health is given us not to waste,
    Health enjoyments must prevail.

T—Call ye Drunkard's life enjoyment
    Set on fire with flames of Hell;
    Then is drinking sweet employment
  . Until woeful want prevail.

D.—Call you Christian life so good
    All unmixed with drink his victual?
    Call you physics understood
    When he cannot taste a little ?

T.—Sure we call the best of physic
    Mix'd with God's sweet loving spirit,
    Cure for care, or sins, or ptysic,
    Full of soul-endowing merit.

D.—Is there aught in all religion
    That can save a soul from death?

T.—Yes, our God, whose saints are legion,
　　Giveth souls immortal breath,
　　Is there not a balm in Gilead ?
　　Not a good physician there ?
　　Little learn'd from Homer's Illiad,
Read God's book with earnest prayer.

D.—Like as Paul so ably argued
　　You are powerful to persuade,
　　Almost turning to be Christian
　　There is weight where truth is said.

T—Turn, be blessed with Christian rules,
　　God can set the captive free ;
　　When he numbereth up his jewels
　　It shall then be well with thee.

March 23, 1880.

REFLECTIONS.

See the drunkard without beauty,
　　Moping sit in Bachus' court
He would shun all moral duty,
　　Who would to such place resort.

On he goes without reflection,
　　Hurrying wildly without fear ;
Wrong and ruin claim connection,
　　Strew with thorns his rough career.

Darkest fate his sense confounding—
　　Oh ! he dare not look ahead ;
Evil language most abounding—
　　Words which should arouse the dead.

Is his heart with passion glowing ?
　　Is there anger in his speech ?
Flames of hell upon him blowing,
　　Placing within misery's reach.

More his foe than friend caressing,
  All unblest his earthly lot,
All unhappy, all unblessing,
  Love nor fortune has he got.

Oh his heart, his heart is riven,
  When his conscience feels its hell,
Hope can never mount to Heaven
  When the *Demon* must prevail.

Demon Drink brings deep damnation,
  Demon Drink lowers every hope;
Brings his brains wild aberration,
  No, he can not, can not stop!

Lo! he's sinking in confusion,
  Dying in his sin and shame;
Hope for him—what vain delusion!
  Love, without a proper name.

March 24, 1880.

THE DRUNKARD'S JOYS.

Behold his joys like shadows fleeting,
  Who, thoughtless pours them down his
    throat;
Nor love nor friendship lend him greeting,
  Like lovely things with happy tho't.

Lo! Love beholds him without wishing
  To be his wife, or paramour;
And friendship is without ambition
  To be acquainted with him more.

Vain are his hopes, vain his enjoyments,
  In narrow'st bounds his soul compress'd,
Living without all good employment,
  As all unblessing, all unblest.

As all unblest and all unblessing,
  Behold him left alone to mope,
The slave of vice, the most bebasing,
  There is for him no certain hope.

No certain hope of good improvement,
  Of virtue forming in his soul,
A well-spring for the heart's belovement,
  Drinking in pleasures heavenly all.

A world of scorn and pride and fashion
  Around—looks freezing coldly on,
Or, whirls in some fantastic passion,
  But seldom lets a heart be known.

The thoughtless ones display their folly,
  The worldly wise that license grant;
The saloonist the liquor poisons,
  To snare, entice to ruin's want.

In ruin's rum, in damning drink, still
  The drunkard drowns all pleasant joys,
All happy hopes—at care he winks, still
  His whole ambition drink employs.

For drink he leaves his wife and children,
  For drink leaves home and oft employ;
The Demon every sense bewildering,
  Oh! is this then the Drunkard's Joy?

The Drunkard dies, and oh! alas! how
   We know his utter deep despair;
The Drunkard dies without his glass too,
   But misery is his portion *where.*

March 26, 1880.

_____

MERCIFUL.

Oh pause, consider, tho'tful ever,
An erring soul is happy never.
Methinks the Drunkard should lie low,
Nor worse, nor better ever know,
Weeds, only weeds, above him grow.

If there's no mercy for the drinker,
How much for reason's lowest thinker?
It would be hard to fix his doom
Midst darkest nights eternal gloom,
With ought of suffering--past the tomb.

As man, when sway'd and teach'd with
   reason,
Makes most of every time and season;
He talks to know, and reads to learn,
That he may every good discern,
All vicious habits he will spurn.

The future clouds o'er headless folly,
The present looks most melancholy,
Beyond a transitory joy,
Who looks not, lets not care annoy,
No heaven-wing'd tho'ts his soul employ.

There is no hope for tho'tless mortal
Beyond the tomb, death's gloomy portal;
Drink not at all, think wisely well,
And let they soul's ambition swell
With happy visions *Immortelle.*

The eye of God is pitiful,
Our Heavenly Father merciful,
And he may take us to his home,
How glorious is his boundless room,
Where he invites us all to come.
March 27, 1880.

TO INIQUITY.

Oh! Iniquity most intense,
Oh! Drunkenness without good sense,
Unto posterity come down
With evil stead of good renown.

Our great forefathers err'd by thee;
Their errors in ourselves we see,
How weak thy were, to thee inclin'd,
So likewise we with erring mind.

Thou sinkest man into the beast,
With every vice by thee increas'd;
Communications most obscene,
Make human nature to look mean.

Tho' loving wisdom teaches some
How easily vice may be o'ercome,
Yet vice inbred into our youth
Opposes wisdom, love and truth.

Oh, Iniquity understood,
Thou art opposed to every good,
The farthest, worst extreme we feel,
With naught to save, with naught to heal.

For every gain thou hast a loss,
For every good thou hast a cross,
For every joy thou hast a sorrow,
And little promise for to-morrow.

Oh never yet wouldst thou befriend,
A hopeful duty to amend ;
Oh never yet would Iniquity
Upon man turn an eye of pity.

March 27, 1880.